EDGE BOOKS™

WILD MOMENTS ON DIRT BIKES

BY M. WEBER

CAPSTONE PRESS

a capstone imprint

Edge Books are published by Capstone Press,
1710 Roe Crest Drive, North Mankato, Minnesota 56003
www.mycapstone.com

Library of Congress Cataloging-in-Publication Data
Library of Congress Cataloging-in-Publication data is available on the Library of Congress website.
ISBN 978-1-5157-7406-8 (library binding)
ISBN 978-1-5157-7410-5 (eBook PDF)

Editorial Credits
Lauren Dupuis-Perez, editor; Sara Radka, designer; Laura Manthe, production specialist

Quote Sources
p.9, "Roger Decoster Interview, Covering 1971 thru 2001." Supercross, June 25, 2012; p.19, "Travis Pastrana
Doubles up, Doubles Down." EPSN, April 28, 2014; p.22, "Connecting People Through News." PressReader.com,
August 12, 2007

Photo Credits
Newscom: John Pyle/Cal Sport Media, cover; Newscom: EPA/Benjamin Manser, 5; Newscom: ZUMAPRESS/
Keystone Pictures USA, 7, 9; Newscom: ZUMAPRESS/Keystone Canada, 8; Newscom: National Motor
Museum/Heritage-Images, 11; Newscom: ZUMAPRESS/Panoramic, 12; Shutterstock: VVKSAM, 15; Newscom:
Studio Milagro/DPPI/Icon SMI, 17; Newscom: ZUMAPRESS/NewSport/Steve Boyle, 18; Newscom:
ZUMAPRESS/Hector Amezcua/Sacramento Bee, 21; Newscom: EPA/Kim Ludbrook, 23; Newscom:
ZUMAPRESS/Brian Ciancio, 25; Newscom: Charles Mitchell/Icon SMI, 27; Shutterstock: Rodrigo Garrido, 29

Graphic elements by Book Buddy Media.

Printed in the United States of America.
010364F17

TABLE OF CONTENTS

DIRT BIKE RACING

Dirt bike racing is fast and dirty. Riders speed over jumps. They soar through the air and slam back to earth. Riders emerge from races covered in the dirt and mud. Unlike other kinds of motorsports, dirt bike riders are not protected by the outer shell of a vehicle. This makes dirt bike racing one of the most physically demanding and dangerous motorsports.

Dirt bike racing is a popular motorsport around the world. In the United States, where it is most popular, this sport is called motocross. There are different types of motocross events. When events are held indoors, riders concentrate on jumps and tricks they perform in the air. Dirt bike races are also held on challenging outdoor courses. No two courses are the same. Dirt bike courses can be anywhere from 1 to 3 miles (1.6 to 4.8 kilometers) long. The **terrain** is rough. Riders often drive over mud and rocks. There are many loops, turns, and hills. Professional riders train for years before they are ready to compete.

terrain—the surface of the land

Though motocross bikes may look the same on the outside, many things have been changed on the inside to make them race ready.

CHAPTER 1

HIDDEN INJURY

Conditions on the track can change depending on the weather. Sometimes the course is dry, and sometimes it is wet. When a course is dry it is easier for riders to reach faster speeds. When a course is wet riders must navigate while slipping and sliding. This is why all riders take practice runs before races.

Roger DeCoster is a well-known motocross racer. In 1978 he was running a test race in Mol, Belgium, and took an unexpected crash. To this day he is not sure what caused him to lose control of his bike. DeCoster seemed fine at first. There were no scratches or marks on the outside of his body. But he could tell something was wrong. He went to the hospital where he learned that his **spleen** had broken into five pieces! He underwent an operation to remove his spleen.

spleen—an organ that is part of the immune system and helps to remove blood cells

Roger DeCoster was inducted into the Motorsports Hall of Fame of America in 1994.

Motocross came to the United States in the 1970s. It began as a popular sport in Europe.

DeCoster considers this 1978 spill his worst accident. He did not stop riding for long, however, as he recalled in an interview, "Surprisingly, two weeks later, I raced and won an international event. It's the biggest pre-Grand Prix event. It's called the 'Easter Trophy.' I won the 250 class, but I felt weird. It felt as though my insides were bouncing around."

OLYMPICS OF DIRT BIKE RACING

The Motocross des Nations is an international race held every year in a new location around the world. It is considered the "Olympics of Motocross." The race merged together with the Trophée des Nations and the Coupe des Nations in 1985 to form a single major event. Riders compete in teams and race to represent their country.

CHAPTER 2

AMERICA ENTERS DIRT BIKE RACING

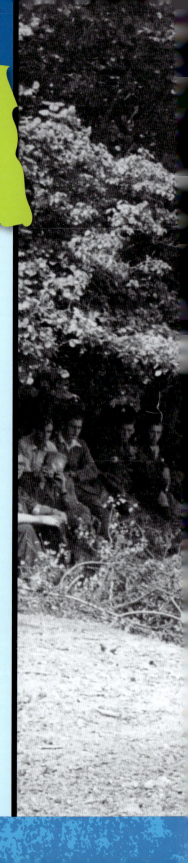

In 1981 dirt bike racing competitions had been taking place around the world for nearly 60 years. But it was still new in the United States. U.S. competitors wanted to show that they could compete with top racers from around the world.

The Trophée des Nations and Motocross des Nations were important European races. The 1981 U.S. team was made up of riders Donnie Hansen, Danny LaPorte, Johnny O'Mara, and Chuck Sun. They were the underdogs of the tournament. When they arrived in Europe they were met with **skepticism** from the European teams.

skepticism—doubt as to the truth of something

The United States won every Motocross des Nations tournament between 1981 and 1993.

Team France won the Motocross des Nations in 2016. It was held in Maggiora, Italy.

In the first round of the Trophée des Nations, each American faced a possible race-ending obstacle. The chains fell from Sun's bike. O'Mara was hit by another rider and pushed from the track, losing valuable time. A rock hit LaPorte in the throat, making it hard to breathe. Hansen's throttle stuck open, and he nearly lost control. This bad luck continued when Sun suffered a crash and ankle injury that took him out of the competition. But his teammates pushed on to victory. They were encouraged by signs from the **pit board** that read "Need Points!" and "Must Pass!" The United States went on to dominate European motocross events for 13 years.

pit board—a board used to relay messages to riders from their pit team, especially before the invention of radios

FLAGS IN DIRT BIKE RACING

Motocross races have flags that give riders information during the race. Different colors have different meanings.

GREEN FLAG
Green means go! It signals the first lap of the race was successful, and the race can continue.

YELLOW
Yellow is the color of caution, telling a rider to slow down or look for an **obstruction** on the course.

RED
Stop! The race must stop immediately as there is a problem on the course.

BLUE FLAG WITH DIAGONAL YELLOW STRIPE
A rider who sees this flag must move over as a rider is passing them. This is used because a rider often cannot see who is approaching from behind or how fast they are coming.

WHITE
White signals the last lap of the race.

CHECKERED FLAG
Every racer's favorite flag, it is dropped when a rider wins the race!

obstruction—a thing that impedes or prevents passage or progress

CHAPTER 3

MORE THAN LUCK

In 1982 Danny "Magoo" Chandler was one of the best riders in the world. In June he won the U.S. Grand Prix in a surprise victory. Chandler won all four events in the Motocross des Nations tournament in Europe, as well. It was a great year, where everything went his way.

It wasn't until a practice run early in 1983 that Chandler's lucky spell was broken. One morning he set off on a practice run in the hills around his home. He had been riding with a friend. The two went different ways. The friend decided to run one more loop before finishing. That's when he found Chandler on the ground. Chandler had crashed his bike and hit his head against a fence post. He had no memory of the accident, and no one knew how long he had been on the ground. After the accident, he could no longer hear from his right ear. It was a frightening time for the racing legend.

Chandler fought to return to motocross. At first he struggled to be the rider he once had been. He remained committed, however. Two years later he won his first race since the accident, on a course in France.

WILD! In 1982 Danny Chandler became the first motocross racer to ever win all four championship races in a single year.

Motocross is a physical and dangerous sport. Up to 95 percent of all motocross riders have sustained injuries while racing.

CHAPTER 4

FOR THE FANS

Dirt bike fans go wild for Stefan Everts. He is considered one of the best dirt bike racers in Europe. Everts has won 10 world titles. But his love for his fans may have cost him a win in 2005.

Everts was leading the pack in the African Grand Prix, when he entered the final stretch. Riders were coming up close behind him. Everts knew his fans were rooting for him. He heard their cheers even over the roar of the engines. To show his thanks, Everts reached one hand into the air to wave to his fans. With only one hand remaining on the handles, he lost control of his bike. Everts fell into the dirt, and his bike flew from beneath him. The **brake lever** on his bike broke. He and his fans had to watch as his competition raced past him, leaving him in the dust.

brake lever—a lever on the handlebar that connects to the brake cable and operates the braking mechanism

Stefan Everts is a successful Belgian motocross racer. His father, Harry Everts, was also a motocross racer.

WILD!

Riders must use the same bike for an entire series. Repairs can only be made between races, so if the bike breaks during one round, the rider cannot continue.

CHAPTER 5

MAKING HISTORY

In 2008 Travis Pastrana was featured in an ESPN documentary about his life called *199 Lives: The Travis Pastrana Story.*

WILD WORLD OF FREESTYLE

Motocross competitions that are only about tricks and jumps are part of freestyle motocross, or FMX. Riders perform daredevil tricks, such as letting their legs fly into the air during a jump. These events are often held indoors on ramps designed specifically for high-flying stunts.

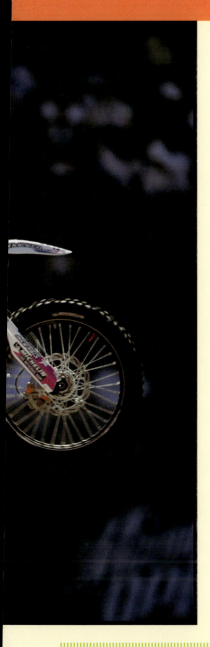

In the wild world of motocross, riders constantly strive to be the fastest. But dirt bikes can do more than race. They are lightweight compared to larger vehicles. Because of this, riders fly high into the air. They show off with tricks and even bigger jumps.

Travis Pastrana is known for always seeking the next thrill. During the 2006 X Games he pulled off a stunt never before completed in competition. His bike roared up a ramp, and he launched into the air. His bike spun backward once, and then twice before his wheels touched the ground. He had pulled off a double back flip. Fans went wild!

When asked about the record-breaking **feat**, Pastrana said, "That adrenaline was pumping like crazy, and to this day I remember every sound, sight, and smell inside the Staples Center that night."

feat—an achievement that requires great courage, skill, or strength

CHAPTER 6

DOWN IN THE MUD

Even when riders know a course, anything can happen on a race day. Sometimes riders will show up to a track that has been dry and baking under the sun. Other days riders show up and find that rain and mud have turned their course into a wet mess.

Ricky Carmichael faced a wet, muddy track one cloudy day in Minnesota in 2007. Carmichael has been called "The Greatest of All Time," and this race may be a good reason why he has earned that nickname. As he took to the muddy course, he started something that had never been done before in U.S. motocross. He pulled to the front of the pack as dirt and water sprayed around him. Then he proved just how good he really was. He **lapped** all the other riders as they struggled to gain **momentum**. This went down in the record books as one of Carmichael's greatest accomplishments. And it was all done in the mud!

lap—to overtake a competitor in a race to become one or more laps ahead

momentum—the force or speed created by movement

Although he is most well known for his record-breaking motocross career, Ricky Carmichael has also competed in NASCAR races.

CHAPTER 7

AIMING HIGH

Motocross riders take big risks. When going over a hill they aim to get as high as possible. This lets them increase their speed. It also means they have farther to fall when they go down the other side. These risks are worth it when it leads to a win. When things go wrong riders can be left feeling the sting of disappointment.

Josh Coppins felt that sting in 2007 after a championship race in the Czech Republic. He went into the race poised to win when disaster struck. Suddenly, he could no longer slow his bike. The brakes had failed. This sent him falling, unable to control the direction or speed of his bike. This setback put him out of the race, and ultimately out of the championship.

After the race he said, "To be honest, things could be better." His short reply is one of a racer determined not to let disappointment keep him from competition. During his recovery he even refused to take painkillers so he could heal faster. He returned to race in the 2008 season.

When Josh Coppins competes in the Motocross des Nations he represents New Zealand, where he is from.

WILD!

Over the years, as motocross has grown to include many kinds of events, riders have become more daring. In FMX riders are always looking for more exciting, and more dangerous, tricks and jumps. These jumps can be as high as 150 feet (46 meters) in the air!

CHAPTER 8

STORMY WEATHER

Unlike other motorsports there is no seatbelt to hold a rider in place on a dirt bike. They must keep control of the bike at high speeds and remain in the seat. This requires a lot of muscle, and sometimes things go wrong.

In 2011 Chad Reed entered a race at Spring Creek Motocross Park in Millville, Minnesota. Reed was in the middle of a race when he encountered an uneven hill. His tires turned sideways as he went up the hill. At the peak he was **ejected** from his seat. He flew into the air while his bike slid down the hill without him. Reed rolled into the grass and then down an incline.

Until his fall he had been the weekend series points leader. Reed didn't want to give up that lead. He quickly recovered. He scrambled to pull his bike back into racing position. Once Reed was back on the seat, he hit the gas and sprang forward to continue the race. He was able to stay in the competition and finished 5th in the end. He proved how tough riders must be to compete in motocross.

eject—to force or throw something out, typically in a violent or sudden way

In 2011 Chad Reed's accomplishments in motocross were recognized by his country. He was named a Member of the Order of Australia.

MOTOCROSS SURFING

Motocross bikes are made for dirt. But motocross star Robbie Maddison likes to push the limits. He decided to take a motocross bike surfing. Maddison and his team spent more than 5,000 hours creating a motocross bike with a large ski attachment. After many tests he was able to create a bike that could drive as far as 15 miles (24 km) across the water. He even took it surfing at Teahupo'o, one of Tahiti's most challenging surf spots.

FOOT OUT OF PLACE

It only takes a small mistake to change the course of a race. Sometimes a minor error can make a rider lose control.

During a 2013 race in Dallas, Texas, Zach Bell's foot slipped slightly, leading to one of the worst wrecks of his career. On a **supercross** course he zipped up a hill and prepared for the second peak when his foot snagged the ground. As soon as his toes touched the earth, his bike began to spin. The forward momentum pushed him and his bike high into the air. Bell flew off the bike in midair. His feet spun above his head, so he had nothing to break his fall. He tumbled to the ground a few feet from where his bike crashed. The medical team rushed to his aid. Thankfully, he was able to stand and walk away on his own. He even raced again in the very next event.

supercross—a motorcycle race held inside a stadium with hairpin turns and high jumps

A company called Dirt Wurx USA is responsible for building most supercross courses in the United States.

WILD! Motocross riders wear a helmet, goggles, pads, and other gear to protect them in falls and crashes.

CHAPTER 10

MAKING A NEW HISTORY

After being the first person to complete a double back flip on a dirt bike, Travis Pastrana retired from racing. But he didn't leave the world of dirt bikes very far behind. He built a park in Maryland called Pastranaland.

Pastranaland includes dirt bike tracks and practice areas. It is where the new stars of motocross come to **hone** their skills. In 2015 Josh Sheehan set out to Pastranaland to attempt something no rider had ever done before. After years of hard work and dedication, he was ready.

Sheehan started on a path surrounded by trees. He revved his engine, and his bike leapt forward. Sheehan raced through the trees toward a ramp that was 37 feet (11.3 m) tall. He soared up and into the air. His bike turned back over front once, twice, and then three times! Sheehan became the first person to complete a triple backflip on a dirt bike! He finished the trick with a perfect landing.

hone—work on and perfect something over a period of time

If a supercross rider lands with both feet off the bike, it is called a "no-footer."

GLOSSARY

brake lever (BRAYK LEV-ur)—a lever on the handlebar that connects to the brake cable and operates the braking mechanism

eject (ee-JEKT)—to force or throw something out, typically in a violent or sudden way

feat (FEET)—an achievement that requires great courage, skill, or strength

hone (HOHN)—work on and perfect something over a period of time

lap (LAP)—to overtake a competitor in a race to become one or more laps ahead

momentum (moh-MEN-tuhm)—the force or speed created by movement

obstruction (ob-STRUHK-shun)—a thing that impedes or prevents passage or progress

pit board (PIT BOHRD)—a board used to relay messages to riders from their pit team, especially before the invention of radios

skepticism (SKEP-teh-si-zuhm)—doubt as to the truth of something

spleen (SPLEEN)—an organ that is part of the immune system and helps to remove blood cells

supercross (SOO-pur-kross)—a motorcycle race held inside a stadium with hairpin turns and high jumps

terrain (tuh-RAYN)—the surface of the land

READ MORE

Cain, Patrick G. *Moto X Best Trick Extreme Summer Sports Zone.* Minneapolis: Lerner Publications, 2017.

Lanier, Wendy Hinote. *Dirt Bikes.* Let's Roll. Mendota Heights, Minn.: Focus Readers, 2017.

Monning, Charles. *Behind the Wheel of a Dirt Bike.* In the Driver's Seat. North Mankato, Minn.: Child's World, 2016.

Schuh, Mari. *The Motorcycle Race.* Let's Race. Mankato, Minn.: Amicus Ink, 2017.

INTERNET SITES

FactHound offers a safe, fun way to find Internet sites related to this book. All of the sites on FactHound have been researched by our staff.

Here's all you do:

Visit *www.facthound.com*

Type in this code: 9781515774068

Check out projects, games and lots more at
www.capstonekids.com

INDEX